# KEVIN'S MYSTERIOUS TUTOR

### A NOVEL BY

## RUSSELL AIUTO

America Star Books
*Frederick, Maryland*

Softcover 9781635082272
PUBLISHED BY AMERICA STAR BOOKS, LLLP
www.americastarbooks.pub
Frederick, Maryland

# CHAPTER ONE

Kevin was doing something of which his mother did not approve.

He was sitting at an umbrella table in front of the coffee shop near his school, reading his English literature textbook, and drinking an iced latte. It was drinking coffee that his mother disapproved of. Somehow, she had gotten the idea that coffee was bad for young boys. It would affect their growth. Kevin, fourteen years old and already five feet eleven inches tall, could not talk his mother out of this old-fashioned belief, one that she had gotten from her mother. In all other things, Kevin thought, his mother was a smart person. For some reason, she clung to grandmother's odd idea.

As he was sitting there, enjoying the warm May afternoon, he realized that a man was standing next to him.

"I beg your pardon," said the man. He was of medium height — not as tall as Kevin — with a neat reddish brown pointed beard, dressed in a tweed sports coat, tan slacks, a light blue shirt, and a red and blue striped tie. He seemed to be over-dressed for the warm day.

"I couldn't help noticing your drink. Pray tell, what is it?" The man had an English accent. He was smiling gently.

"Oh," said Kevin, who was not comfortable with strangers, but replied nonetheless, "it's an iced latte."

"Latte?" the man said. "That means 'milk' in Italian, does it not?"

"I don't know. I know Spanish, but I don't know the word for 'milk' in Italian," Kevin said. "I suppose it is, though. The Spanish for 'milk' is 'leche' and that sounds a lot like 'latte'."

"Brilliant! I do believe I'll purchase one of those." The man turned and entered the coffee shop. In a few minutes, he returned, holding an iced latte. "Do you mind if I join you? Very pleasant day, isn't it?"

"No, I don't mind," Kevin said.

"Jolly good. By the way, you really should learn Italian. Wonderful language. Very musical, very descriptive."

"My school doesn't teach it," Kevin said.

"No matter. Teach yourself. I did. Very easy to do, you know. One can teach one's self almost anything, if one wishes."

"Well, I'll give it a try sometime."

"My name's William. You must be Kevin," the man said.

Kevin was startled. "How did you know my name?"

"Oh, quite simple, really. I'm your tutor. I was told to look for a lad about six feet tall, reading a textbook, and drinking coffee. Kevin. Not a name I've ever encountered. Is it Irish?"

"I think so. My father is Irish, and my mother is Scottish. I didn't know I had a tutor."

"Indeed you do. Yes, Kevin does sound Irish. I'm very interested in names."

Kevin frowned at William. "Who sent you? I mean, who hired you to be my tutor?"

"Oh, I haven't the faintest. I'm just sent where I'm told. You are studying English literature, aren't you? That's my specialty, you see. I was told you were going to have a special course of instruction in the subject, come this fall, and I'm here to prepare you for success."

"Yes, I am. It's an Advanced Placement class. 'Composition and English Literature' it's called."

"Well, I'm sure you'll do smashingly with my help. When would you like to start? We could meet here, if you wish. Very comfortable here, I would say. Is tomorrow too soon?"

"But who's paying you? I don't think my parents can afford a tutor. And I'm not sure I even need one."

"Don't bother yourself with that. It's all taken care of. As for needing a tutor, think of it more as my being your mentor, and you, my apprentice." William drank the last of his latte and stood up. "Well, I must be off. Tomorrow, then. Say, after school? Two-thirty?"

Kevin looked at the pleasant man, as if trying to place him. He looked a bit familiar, but he couldn't remember where he might have seen him before. "I guess two-thirty would be okay."

"Splendid. See you tomorrow, Kevin. Oh, by the way. Are there any plays in that volume of yours?" he said, pointing to Kevin's textbook.

"Oh, yes. *Romeo and Juliet*. I was just reading it."

"Splendid. Could you finish it? We'll begin our lessons tomorrow with that. One of my favorites, *Romeo and Juliet*. Well, cheerio. Until tomorrow."

Kevin, not at all sure of what had just taken place, watched as William walked jauntily away.

It was after four by the time Kevin got home. His mother was peeling potatoes over the sink. Without looking over her shoulder, she said, "Good day?"

"It was alright. Don't forget. I have a game tonight. Is my uniform clean?"

"Yes, it's clean. You don't think that I'd let Longport's star second baseman play with a dirty uniform, do you?"

Kevin got a soft drink from the refrigerator. "Mom, did you and Dad get me a tutor?"

"You want a tutor?" asked his mother.

"No, I said did you get me one. You know, sign me up for tutoring."

"Heavens, no! What ever for? Your grades are fine. You don't need a tutor. Besides, right now, with your sister in college, I don't think that we could afford one."

"Well," said Kevin, "this man came by while I was … while I was just sitting near school and said he was my tutor. He was going to tutor me in English Lit."

His mother finished the last potato and turned to him, drying her hands on her apron. "Oh, your English teacher — what's her name? — Mrs. Frederick, probably found some volunteer and suggested that this man — this tutor — help you out. I suppose she wants you to do well in the Fall. What was he like, this tutor? Probably a retired professor or something."

"He could have been, but I don't think he's old enough to be retired. He was late forties, maybe around fifty. English. He had an English accent."

"Well, if you think he might help you, take advantage of it. Wouldn't hurt. As your father would say, you might learn something."

Sometimes Mrs. Ryan worried about Kevin. He was so different from the other tenth graders she met while working in the high school library. He didn't seem to care about current styles in clothes. He did very well in his classes. She would have thought that he would have been teased by other students for being so indifferent to the things that most teenagers liked.

But he wasn't teased. He was well liked, although his only really close friend was Julia Black. Perhaps, thought Mrs. Ryan, it was because he was such an outstanding athlete — a member of the varsity teams in football, basketball, and baseball. He was naturally graceful, and sports came easily to him, or so it seemed to his fellow students. In reality, Kevin practiced very hard, always trying to improve some detail or other on how best to play the game. Still, his mother worried. Some how, being an outstanding student and athlete should make some kids jealous or resentful, but they weren't. When she expressed her worries to Kevin's father, Mr. Ryan replied, "It's because he's such a classy kid. After all, he's pleasant and polite, good at everything he does, he doesn't brag or lord it over other kids — he's just classy. Sometimes I think he's forty years old, rather than fourteen."

"Well, I wish he was a little bit more … normal," said Mrs. Ryan.

"Oh, he's normal all right," Mr. Ryan said, laughing. "He just doesn't care what people think of him, but he thinks well about everybody else. The kid could be a great politician someday, Agnes. He can charm the pants off anybody without their knowing he's doing it. I don't know where he got it — not from me, I'll tell ya."

"Not from my side of the family," Mrs. Ryan said. "Do you think they switched babies on us in the hospital?"

Mr. Ryan laughed. "No, I don't think so. Somewhere along the way he decided for himself what's important and what's unimportant, and he's stuck with it. The problem we have, I think, is showing him how proud we are of him without letting it go to his head."

"Jim Ryan! You know as well as I do that there's nothing we could do that would make him behave badly. It's just not in his nature."

Mr. Ryan nodded. "Yeah, you're right. Now, what's this about a tutor?"

# CHAPTER TWO

"Ah, Kevin, early! Good, good. Punctuality is an admirable trait. Now, why don't I fetch us two of those delightful lattes, whilst you review the opening of the play. You did read the play, didn't you?"

Kevin, who had arrived at the coffee shop fifteen minutes early, nodded.

"Splendid! Go on. That opening speech of the Chorus. I'll just be half a minute, about the time it'll take you to go through it." William briskly went into the coffee shop.

He returned with two iced lattes with straws sticking up through the plastic lids. "There. Proper stimulation for our work." He placed one of the lattes in front of Kevin's book.

Kevin hesitated.

"Well, read on, my lad, read on. Give me the speech, and then we'll parse it."

"I'm sorry," said Kevin. "What do you mean?"

"Parse it. Take it apart, as it were. Analyze it."

"But don't you need a copy of the play?"

"Oh, good heavens, no! Know every word of it. Go on, go on."

Kevin read the fifty or so lines aloud. "Now," said William, "what is this gentleman telling us? Or, rather, what is the author having this gentleman tell us?"

"I guess he's getting us ready for the play. You know, telling us that there are these two families who hate each other, and that nothing good can come of it."

William smiled broadly. "Exactly! And, pray-tell, what does the author mean when he speaks of Romeo and Juliet as 'star-crossed lovers'? What does that tell us about the play?"

Kevin thought for a minute. "I don't know. Does it mean that they have bad luck or something like that?"

"That's it. Bad luck. Misfortune. But, you see, since they are 'crossed up' by the stars, so to speak, it is misfortune not of their own doing. Do you see what I mean? What will happen to them will not be the result of their actions, but of fate, of an array of events completely out of their hands."

"But that doesn't seem fair," Kevin said. "People should be able to take charge of their own lives. They shouldn't be … victims of … bad luck."

"Ah, very good. Quite right. But, you see, they are. That's why the author called the play a tragedy. What do you think a tragedy is?"

"I guess it's a story where things end badly. The opposite of a happy ending."

"Would people who, let us say, spend their lives in boredom, would they be tragic figures?"

"They could be. I guess being always bored is as bad as being dead."

"Very good. But, you see, to be *real* tragedy, the bad ending has to be in complete contrast to the happy ending. To fall only a few feet is an accident. To fall from a mountain top is a tragedy. Do you see what I mean?"

Kevin had never had a teacher like this. He was so excited, and he made what he was teaching exciting. His eyes flashed with enthusiasm, and he made this small part of the play as interesting as a two-hour movie.

"Yes, I see what you mean," Kevin said. "It's all the more tragic because young love has so much to look forward to, and to be robbed of it by bad luck makes it even worse."

William beamed. "That, my lad, is the essence of tragedy!" He finished his latte with a loud slurp.

"How do you know this play so well, William?" Kevin asked.

"Well, you see, Kevin, I have lived with this play — and with many others — for a very long time. I was once an actor, you see. In this play, for instance, I, at various times, portrayed the Chorus, I was Benvolio, and as I got older, I played Friar Laurence. Is it any wonder that I know the play by heart?"

Kevin had a sudden thought. "Do you know *all* of Shakespeare's plays that well?"

William smiled. "Every one," he said. "Every one."

# CHAPTER THREE

The ball had hit a stone and bounced right into Kevin's face. It hit him right on the bridge of his nose, and as he fell to the ground, his hands covering his face, blood seeped between his fingers.

The coach was kneeling over him, pressing his handkerchief against Kevin's nose. "Bend forward, Kevin. Hold your head towards your knees. Let's see if we can stop the bleeding."

An hour later, the emergency room doctor pulled back the curtain and spoke to Kevin's mother. "Well, Mrs. Ryan, it's a good old fashioned broken nose. I've straightened it back, so he'll be okay. He'll have a couple of black eyes for a couple of weeks, but, other than that, he'll be fine. He may need these pain pills for today and tomorrow, but after that it'll just be a little sore."

"Thank goodness," said Mrs. Ryan. "I suppose he should stop playing baseball for awhile?"

The doctor smiled. "I think that'd be a good idea, at least for a few weeks. It's probably not a good idea to risk his being hit in the nose again. After that, he'll just have to be careful about bad hops."

Kevin felt terrible. His face ached, and he was sleepy from the pain pills. He spent most of the next day in bed, getting up only to go to the bathroom. He ate very little, since his face felt stiff and it hurt to chew food.

The following day, Kevin returned to school, a bandage across his nose and the areas around his eyes a dark purple. He wore sunglasses. After school, he made his way to the coffee shop. He and William had not scheduled their tutoring sessions. Kevin assumed that William would be there every day.

When he got to the coffee shop, William was at their table, sitting under the umbrella, sipping an iced latte.

"Kevin, my dear boy, what on Earth happened to you?"

Kevin took off his sunglasses and grinned at William. "Bad hop," Kevin said.

"I beg your pardon?"

"Bad hop. The ball hit a stone or something and hit me in the face."

"What ball? I don't follow."

"You know, a baseball. I bent down to field it, and it skipped over my glove and hit me right on the bridge of my nose. It broke my nose, but the doctor straightened it. I'll look like this for a couple of weeks."

William was clearly puzzled. "So, this happened, I take it, during some sort of game?"

Now Kevin was puzzled. "Yes, a baseball game. I play baseball three nights a week. I play second."

"Well, well. I see. Baseball. You must explain the game to me at some point in our studies. I do hope that it's not too painful."

"Kinda, at least yesterday. But it feels better today. I'm okay."

"Perhaps we had better postpone our studies until another day."

"I'd just as soon we did," Kevin said. "I didn't have a chance to re-read Act One."

"No matter. It can wait. After all, the play is four hundred years old. Perhaps we can just chat for a bit. Enjoy the fine weather. Can I get you a latte, pray tell?"

"No thanks, William." Kevin paused. "William, where do you come from?"

"Come from? That should be obvious. From England, you know, that 'sceptered isle'."

"Yes, I know that, but where do you live? I mean, where do you live now?"

"Ah, I see. Well, most recently, Canada. Currently, I reside in a charming set of rooms over Black's hardware store. Very comfortable quarters, I can assure you."

"Do you have a family?"

"Indeed I do. A fine, stout wife and two charming daughters. They, however, are in England. My stay in your lovely country is temporary, you see."

Kevin could not make sense of this strange man. "When do you go back to England?"

"Ah, a very good question. In a nutshell, when my work here is done. When you and I have mastered *Romeo and Juliet*, and perhaps another play. I'm partial to *Hamlet*. When I'm certain that you are in fine form, I shall move on. Perhaps I will return to England. I may go back to Canada. My schedule, you see, is quite free and open."

Kevin was about to ask another question, but William stood up before he could ask it. "But enough of this. You must go home and rest. We'll resume tomorrow, if you feel up to it. If you can't make it, don't concern yourself. I will wait for you, refresh myself, read a bit of your local paper, and return again. Well, I must be off. Cheerio, and do get some rest."

And with that, William walked off with his usual jaunty step.

# CHAPTER FOUR

Black's Hardware Store had been since 1932, and it had changed little in those sixty and more years. Kevin went there often, since his best friend from school, Julia Black, worked there for her father, just as her father had worked for his, and his father before that.

After leaving the coffee shop, Kevin decided to drop by Black's. As he expected, Julia was there, posted at the cash register. "Kevin," she said, "look at you! Let me see!" Kevin removed his sunglasses.

Julia laughed. "You look like a raccoon. Those are beautiful shiners." Kevin grinned sheepishly. He knew that Julia was teasing him, and that she wasn't being cruel.

"I knew that you must have been really hurt. You don't miss school very often. When you weren't there yesterday and today, I knew it must be painful. Is it better?"

"Oh, yeah. Much better. Just a little sore. Listen, Julia. What can you tell me about the man who lives upstairs? William? I don't know his last name."

"Not much. He's a funny kind of man. Always smiling and pleasant, but he only goes out between two and four-thirty in the afternoon."

"That's because he's my tutor. He's tutoring me in English Lit. We meet at the coffee shop and study Shakespeare."

Mr. Black approached them. "Dad," Julia said, "William is Kevin's tutor. Did you know that?"

"He is? No, I didn't. Wouldn't surprise me, though. He seems like a teacher, or a professor of some kind. I love the way he talks. Very British, very proper." Mr. Black began to duplicate some keys for a customer, the key machine whirring away.

"What's his last name?" Kevin asked.

"Let me see — can't think of it at the moment. Oh, I remember. Kemp. William Kemp. I wouldn't know that, except

I had him sign a lease. He's only here for a month. Just brought two suitcases with him." Mr. Black finished duplicating the keys. "Funny that he'd only be here for a month, just to tutor you, Kevin."

"Maybe he's doing something else as well," Julia said. "You know, maybe he's a writer or something and needs a quiet place to work."

"That would make sense," Mr. Black said. "Writers are funny people to begin with, don't you think?"

"I wonder what he's working on," Kevin said.

"Some masterpiece or other," Mr. Black said. He looked up at Kevin. "Looks like that ball really got you, Kevin. Hope it doesn't hurt too much."

"As long as I don't blow my nose," Kevin said.

# CHAPTER FIVE

"So, Kevin, my lad, recount for me as best you can the plot of the play, and I will stop you at one point and another. We will then examine how well our author was able to construct the story. Begin."

"Well, Romeo thinks that he is in love with Rosalind, but it's just a crush…"

William held up his hand. "I beg your pardon. 'Crush?' Pray tell, what is a 'crush'?"

"Oh. You know, an attraction. Not real love."

"Very interesting use of a word. I must remember that. Go on. Forgive the interruption."

"Well, Romeo is being teased by his friends, Benvolio and Mercutio, and this servant comes upon them. He's delivering invitations to a party being given by Old Capulet, Juliet's father, but he can't read, so he stops and asks for help. Even though the Capulets and Romeo's family, the Montagues, are enemies, Mercutio thinks that it's a good idea for them to go, and the stupid servant who can't read invites them."

"Stop there. What do you make of the servant who can't read and stops to ask for help?"

Kevin was puzzled. "What do I make of it? Nothing, I guess. It's just a servant who can't read that happens to bump into the three of them."

"Ah, the important word is 'happens" isn't it? What would have happened if the servant had asked someone else for directions?"

"Oh, I see what you mean! Romeo would never have gone to the Capulet party and he would never have met Juliet."

"Exactly! Don't you see? This is the first time of many in the play where chance plays an important part in the story. Right from the beginning, our author has constructed a plot where accidents construct how the story will proceed."

Kevin paused. "Why do you refer to 'the author' and not Shakespeare?" Kevin asked.

"A habit, merely a habit. One must be impersonal when examining literature, Kevin, and not worry about who or what the author is."

They continued on for another hour, Kevin telling the story and William interrupting him with questions about the plot of the play, and about the personalities of the characters.

They had gotten as far as the first meeting between Romeo and his friend and teacher, Friar Laurence, when William said, "Enough for today. We'll resume tomorrow, shall we? I am pleased with your progress, Kevin. You are a fine scholar."

As William rose to leave, Kevin suddenly said, "William, is your last name Kemp?"

William smiled. "I have been known to respond to that name."

"I was wondering," Kevin said, "about what you do when you're not meeting with me. Are you a writer or something?"

"Writer, actor, yes, I keep busy."

"What do you write?"

"Words. Words, words."

"I mean, what kind of stuff do you write?"

"Poetry. Drama. Of all those matters that uplift the soul and explain our lives. I am compelled to examine the hearts of men and women. I believe there is a modern phrase for my work — 'to see what makes them tick,' don't you see?"

"Isn't that what Shakespeare did?" Kevin asked.

"I believe he did, Kevin. But, enough of this, I must be off. Tomorrow, then. Same time."

And with that bouncy walk of his, William went off.

# CHAPTER SIX

Kevin had arrived at Black's Hardware Store a few minutes after eight o'clock, closing time on a Friday night. Mr. Black had just let the clerks out the back door and was turning off lights as he moved to the front of the store, while Julia was putting money and receipts from the cash register into a cloth bank bag.

"So," said Mr. Black, "it's not an R-rated movie, is it? Your mother has strong feelings about that, Julia."

"Oh, Daddy, don't be an old grump. It's a perfectly harmless movie about space aliens."

"Sounds awful," Mr. Black said.

"Well, it's not Shakespeare," said Kevin.

"Bet you'll be glad when you have your driver's license, won't you Kevin? Won't have to have your girl friend's old man drive you everywhere."

"It would be nice," Kevin said.

As they were heading for Mr. Black's car, Julia's father said, "Speaking of Shakespeare, Kevin, your tutor has turned out not to be such a hermit after all. Seems he's been spending his evenings at Malloy's Bar and Grill. He's quite the boy, I hear, telling stories and keeping the regulars entertained."

"He must be lonely," Julia said.

"Well, not anymore," her father said.

Mr. Black dropped them off, and just before eleven o'clock he was waiting for them in the parking lot across the street from the movie theatre. "Good movie?" he asked as Julia and Kevin both got into the front seat with him.

"It was all right," Kevin said.

"Actually, Daddy, it was awful. Just one creepy thing after another."

They drove along for a few minutes. As they stopped at a red light, Mr. Black noticed a figure sitting on a bench near the bus stop. "Isn't that our Mr. Kemp?"

Sitting erectly on the bench, his hands on his knees, was William. His eyes were closed and he had a serene smile on his face.

"Oh, let's give him a lift, Daddy," Julia said.

Mr. Black pulled over. He rolled down the window on Kevin's side and leaned forward. "Give you a lift, Mr. Kemp?"

William opened his eyes. "How very kind of you. But I do believe I will walk to my quarters. It is a lovely evening, is it not? A shame to forego an opportunity for exercise."

"Are you sure you're all right, William?" Kevin asked.

"Ah, perfectly fine, my boy. Fine as can be."

Julia touched Kevin's shoulder and whispered, "Do you think he may have had a little too much to drink?"

Kevin whispered back. "I think so, but it's hard to tell." He turned back to William, still sitting on the bench, smiling. "William, it is rather late. You'd be better off waiting until tomorrow when it's light for your walk. You can't tell what could happen this late."

"There are more things on heaven and earth than are dreamt of in your philosophy, Horatio."

Mr. Black said, "What'd he say?"

"I think it's from *Hamlet*," Kevin said. Turning back to William, Kevin said, "I really think you should come along with us, William."

"The fault, Dear Brutus, is not in the stars. It is in ourselves."

"Now what?" Mr. Black said.

"*Julius Caesar*, I think," Kevin said.

Julia was giggling. "You'd better give him a hand, Kevin," Mr. Black said. "He may be able to spout Shakespeare, but I'm not sure he can walk."

Kevin got out of the car and walked over to William. "Really, William, you should come along with us."

"Very kind of you, yes, but, really Kevin, I prefer walking home. I must needs rest a bit before I proceed. I assure you, I have not had too much Rhenish, and that that I have consumed will soon be gone, floating into the ether. Go, go, with my thanks. I shall be fine. The night is wondrous still, the stars do shine, and I am content to sit a spell."

"If you're sure …"

"Quite sure. I will see you on the morrow, and we will delve once more into the matters of ancient Verona. Be gone, be gone." He was smiling.

"Okay. See you tomorrow. G'night, William."

"Good night, my lad. Good night." With that, William closed his eyes and folded his hands across his stomach.

Kevin returned to the car. "He says he's okay, and he'd rather walk. I think he's all right. He certainly doesn't sound drunk."

Mr. Black laughed. "If that's what he wants. He seems like the kind of fellow who knows how to handle the stuff. Well, let's get the two of you home. I'll drive back this way after I drop you off, Kevin, and check on him."

Thirty minutes later, Mr. Black drove by the bus stop. William was gone.

# CHAPTER SEVEN

Kevin was standing behind Julia as she worked at her computer. "What I'll do is do a Google search for 'William Kemp' and see if your tutor is famous."

She typed in *William Kemp* into the Google box and clicked *go*. A long list appeared on the screen.

"I think we'll have to narrow it down," Kevin said. "Try *William Kemp, Actor*."

Julia corrected the Google box and clicked *go* again. This time an entry appeared that said *Will Kemp, Elizabethan Actor*. She double-clicked the entry. On the screen appeared a biography of Will Kemp, 1555-1603. They read it.

Will Kemp had been the principal comic actor in Shakespeare's theatre company, and was known for his dancing ability. He once danced backwards all the way from London to Norwich as a stunt. The biography said that Kemp often improvised lines in a play in which he was acting, and that Shakespeare didn't like it. The author of the biography suggested that Hamlet's famous speech to the players was really a criticism of Kemp's tendency to improvise — "and let your players speak no more than what is written down for them" — and the audience knew what he was referring to.

"Do you think that this is the ancestor of your William?" Julia asked.

"It doesn't sound much like William. If genes are important, I don't think our present William Kemp has the ones that Will Kemp had."

They continued to search the other Google entries, but they were much the same as the biography they had read.

"Well, Kevin, the present William Kemp is not famous enough to have anything about him on the Web. Maybe he's just what he says he is. An actor and a writer and a teacher who hasn't been much of a success."

"I guess so," Kevin said. "But he's so *smart*, and he's so mysterious that I'm surprised. I guess I had hoped that he was famous."

"You know, Kevin, there's another possibility. Maybe his real name isn't William Kemp."

# CHAPTER EIGHT

At the very moment that Julian and Kevin were again surfing the web, Mr. Black received a telephone call at the hardware store.

"John?" The voice on the other end of the line was Dr. Emerson, a long-time friend of Mr. Black's. "Paul here. Listen, do you have a tenant by the name of William Kemp?"

"I sure do, Paul. What's up?"

"Well, he's with me. Sheriff Krumm called me. It seems that this Mr. Kemp or whatever his name is walked away from St. Elizabeth's Hospital in DC. One of the patrol cars saw him last night, sitting on a bench near a bus stop, talked to him, and brought him in. He hadn't done anything wrong — maybe a little too much to drink — but he couldn't answer the officer's questions very well. Anyway, they brought him in, checked to see if he was wanted anywhere, and it came up that he had walked away from St. Elizabeth's. Now, he was a voluntary patient there, so he hadn't done anything wrong, but it's standard procedure to report patients that walk away. They kept him overnight and called me this morning. So, I went down and got him. Krumm thought that I could figure out what to do with him."

"He seems perfectly normal to me, Paul. He's a little eccentric, but he seems okay. What's the problem?"

"Well, could you come over to my office? He's got a rather strange story, and I think that he needs to talk to somebody who knows him."

"I'll be right over," Mr. Black said.

It was only a five minute walk to Dr. Emerson's office. When he arrived, William was sitting in front of Dr. Emerson's desk, drinking a cup of coffee, and chatting away as if he were making a social visit.

"Ah, my good innkeeper! So good to see you. It seems that I have confused the good doctor here, to say nothing of the very pleasant sheriff I met earlier."

"Mr. Kemp …"

"Oh, come now, call me William."

"Okay, William. Now, what's going on?"

Dr. Emerson took over. "Your friend, William, has a rather strange tale to tell. I thought I'd let you hear it, and then we could decide how we could best help him."

"Yes, I am afraid my tale is a bit strange. I am not permitted to share it widely, but it seems that my fate is in the hands of the good doctor here, as well as you, my friend. Let me recount for you how it came to be that I was in hospital in your nation's capital. You see, I suddenly found myself on the streets of Washington, feeling very disoriented. For awhile, I wasn't sure who I was, or where I was. This always happens on occasions such as these."

"What occasions?" asked Mr. Black.

"More of that later. I shall explain at length. When I am so disoriented, I normally proceed to some place of healing — a hospital or a physician or, on rare occasions, a church. This is what I did. I found a very helpful young man who listened to my plight — that I was not feeling myself and needed attention — and he directed me to St. Elizabeth's. I understand that it is an institution for madmen, but, no matter, I was certain that they could help me find my feet, so to speak. They did indeed. I described my problem. I wasn't sure who I was or where I was. Very skillfully, a very pleasant young woman — a physician, no less! — discussed my problem with me, and suggested that I remain with them for a period, until I could resolve these issues.."

"I take it that you did. Resolve the issues, I mean," said Mr. Black.

"I did indeed. In a few days, I was myself again. And, I might add, it was a very productive few days, for it allowed me to observe the customs and people of the day. I am a quick study, I must modestly admit, so it wasn't long before I understood that I was in a most advanced and amazing time."

"I don't follow you," said Mr. Black. "What do you mean by an 'advanced and amazing time'?"

"This is where it gets good," said Dr. Emerson. "Tell him, William."

"You see, I am a bit of a time traveler, if you like. I seem to come and go, visiting different ages. It is most disconcerting. I am never sure where I am. Fortunately, after a day or two — several days, at the most — I quite understand where I am and what is expected of me. It is that shock of entry that causes the problems. Hence, my visit to St. Elizabeth's was an attempt to allow me to enter my — as it were — new time."

Mr. Black looked at Dr. Emerson. He turned to William and said, "Uh ... Mr. Kemp ..."

"William."

"Uh, yes, William — have you ... visited many different times?"

"Oh, good lord, not many. I believe this is my fifth — or is it sixth? — time. I believe I am getting quite proficient at these visits. You see, here I am, explaining everything to you in the most understandable terms. But, pray tell, I would prefer that you not mention my visiting from another time. Others might not be as perceptive as yourselves, and confusion could ensue. In particular, I must explain this myself to Kevin. It would damage our mentor-pupil relationship if he were to learn from someone else that I have come here from another time."

Dr. Emerson looked at William in a very serious way. "Very well, William, but you must know that we find this hard to believe. We'll keep your secret, but you must assure us that you mean no one no harm. We have to know that you're being truthful with us."

"Oh, goodness, of course! My visits are always to do good, in whatever small way I can. I can assure you that I will teach

Kevin, carry out my writing, and leave you, none the worse. I give you my word."

Mr. Black turned to Dr. Emerson. "Paul, that's good enough for me. You satisfied?"

Dr. Emerson nodded. "Sure. Good luck, William. Your secret is safe with us."

William sighed in relief. "My thanks, gentlemen. I do not usually reveal my origin on these visits, and I am most grateful. Now, if I may know the time?"

"Two-fifteen," Dr. Emerson said.

"Oh, I must be off. I have my session with Kevin at half past the hour. Adieu, gentlemen. And thank you so much."

After William had left, Mr. Black asked Dr. Emerson, "Do you think it's all right, I mean, our letting him go? He's not all there, you know."

"He seems harmless," Dr. Emerson said. "I don't think he'll be a problem."

"I've got to tell Jim Ryan, though. After all, it's his son the loony is teaching."

"Yes, by all means. But, you know, I'm inclined to keep our word about what he's told us — except for Jim of course. He seems like a really nice man — obviously he's very bright — and I kind of like him. What do you think, John? Should we keep it quiet?"

Mr. Black was silent. "Well, come to think of it, I'm not sure that Jim should know — at least for right now, until we see how he behaves. I don't see any harm in letting Mr. Kemp do whatever it is he's doing. But I tell you, Paul, that was the strangest thing I ever heard. You know, I think that — at least for awhile — I believed him."

"That's funny," said Dr. Emerson. "So did I."

# CHAPTER NINE

"This is extremely awkward, Kevin, extremely awkward. I am sure that you have many questions."

The day was bright, and Kevin, facing the sun, was glad that he was still wearing his sunglasses to hide his fading black eyes. "You don't have to explain anything to me, William. You have a right to keep stuff to yourself."

"What has Mr. Black told you?"

"Only that you were in a hospital for awhile. That you felt that you didn't need to stay there and left. That's all."

"Yes, quite right. Well, I will attempt to explain. You see, every so often I am sent on a mission. As a matter of fact, *you* are my current mission."

Kevin interrupted. "Who sends you on these missions?"

"Ah. Excellent question. The truth is, I don't know. One moment I am where I usually am, and the next, I find myself in a strange place. Under those circumstances, you can see that I would be somewhat disoriented."

"I guess I would be, too," Kevin said. "How often does this happen."

William paused. "That, too, is an excellent question. My answer will confound you, I'm afraid. About every eighty years. This is the fourth time."

Kevin looked alarmed.

"Yes," William said, "I note your disbelief. It is unbelievable, is it not? Allow me to elaborate."

"I think you should," Kevin said.

"Suspend belief for a moment. You see, I was born in 1564. I died in 1616. I am, therefore, an angel, a ghost, a specter — whatever one chooses to call a creature that reappears after death. My memory of those almost four hundred years since my death is vague, a variety of what might be called 'suspended animation.' No recollection of the many years between ... visits, I suppose you'd call them, and only a vague sense of well-being, of contentment. Somehow, I sense that heavenly (if that's what it is) existence between these visits to the living world are happy and productive, but one cannot be sure of that. I just, as I say, 'sense' it."

Kevin looked at William with widened eyes. "You're William Shakespeare, aren't you?"

"Yes, quite so. I chose the name of one of the actors in my company, The Chamberlain's Men. I could not very well introduce myself with my true name. You would have considered me mad, a lunatic."

"William," Kevin said, "I think a lot of you, but why shouldn't I consider you a lunatic now?"

William laughed. "You should, Kevin, my lad, you certainly should. But my mission is too important to worry about that. Allow me to continue."

"All right," said Kevin.

"These missions, as I've called them, always amount to the same task. I am sent to interact with a young man. You are the youngest, but none of the four has been older than nineteen years of age. The intent of these assignments, as I understand them, is to encourage each young man to pursue a life of (if you will excuse the immodesty) Shakespearean scholarship. Why this is important to whomever or whatever sends me, I cannot say, only that it is so."

"So, I'm to grow up and be a scholar. A professor of some kind? Not a lawyer."

"I don't know. None of your three predecessors were professors. They all had professions quite different from one another. Of course, one was rich, so earning a living was not a problem for him. I don't know your fate. I only know that somehow you will fulfill the destiny for which I have been sent. Why this should be important, I cannot tell you."

"What am I supposed to do? Are you going to teach me everything about your plays, and then I'm supposed to write books about them?"

"I believe that that is the desired outcome. But there is one other matter. These visits of mine — by the conventional standards of time — are only of a month in duration. Eight days of that allotment has already passed. It is unlikely that I can teach you everything about my work in a mere twenty-two days. Also, here is the matter I needs must point out to you. After I have gone, you will not remember my visit."

Kevin frowned. "That doesn't make sense, William. Too many people have met you. That's impossible."

"Ah, I am afraid it is not impossible. None of you — not the charming Julia, her kind father, you — none will remember me. Oh, you will remember being taught by a very strange tutor, and the others will recall an interesting visitor, but none of you will remember me as William Shakespeare, who somehow came to Earth for a month. Collectively, your memories will selectively recall reasonable explanations, not, I fear, supernatural ones. And that is as it should be."

Kevin was silent for a moment. "In that case, I have an idea. We should put on one of your plays while you're here, and you should direct it. I mean, who could not want to be in one of Shakespeare's plays, directed by William Shakespeare himself?"

For once, William was speechless. "But, my dear boy, three weeks is not sufficient time to prepare a production of a play. I appreciate the honor, but it is, I fear, an insurmountable task."

"So we don't have it ready before you ... disappear. We would be far enough into it that we could finish getting it ready ourselves. Besides, can you think of a better way of making me into a Shakespearean scholar in only three weeks?"

William smiled. "Kevin, my lad, you are a remarkable young man. We could undertake what you suggest, I suppose. We could produce *Romeo and Juliet*. I can see you as Romeo, and the winsome Julia as Juliet. But, alas, I fear that the idea is not only impractical, but — forgive me — somewhat silly."

Kevin was offended. "What's so silly about it?"

"Kevin, my lad, there are certain requirements for presenting one of my plays. I have heard that they are popular with amateur theatre groups, and I am flattered. But it is quite incorrect to say that *any* Shakespeare is better than *no* Shakespeare. There are demands on those who act my plays, demands that require levels of experience in the dramatic arts that are the result of years of effort. I won't damage your critical judgment by encouraging you to participate in anything less than a professional effort. Tell me, have you ever appeared upon a stage?"

"Well, no. Well, when I was in elementary school. I played a rabbit. But I would like to. And I've never seen a Shakespeare play."

"Hmm. Could it be that my role in your development is to produce not a scholar, but an actor? A very fine, insightful actor of Shakespeare? Intriguing thought. Well, for our purposes, let us forego your debut upon the stage for the present and work on understanding the play scripts themselves. Be not disheartened. Whatever your fate, our work will result in your considerable accomplishments."

Disappointment was clearly on Kevin's face. "If you say so, but it seemed like a great idea to me."

"Oh, it is, it is! Only there is so much to do in a mere three weeks that I must decline your kind offer. You must remember that there is school to attend, games to play, and — what is it that you call the cinema? Movies? — yes, movies to see. Life must proceed as normally as possible, or you will look back on my visit with more confusion than it will already engender."

"Okay. Where are we?"

"Ah, we are now about to embark on the balcony scene. The first one. 'What light through yonder window breaks?' Let us examine this. I understand that it has become quite famous."

# CHAPTER TEN

"Tell me, Kevin. What do your fellows think of my work?"

"Sorry? What do you mean, William?"

William Shakespeare leaned back in his chair. "I mean, dear boy, do your fellow students find my plays interesting?"

Kevin was flustered for a moment. He didn't want to hurt William's feelings, but he knew that he had to be honest.

"Well, they find your plays kinda ... difficult."

"Is that another way of suggesting that they find them dull?"

"Yes, I suppose so. The language is so hard. I don't think that they understand what the characters are saying. You know, the poetry and stuff."

"This we must discuss! Allow me to renew our refreshments, and we will pursue this." William went into the coffee shop and returned with two iced lattes. "Now, let us examine the issue of language."

"Okay," Kevin said.

"For example, this speech. Friar Laurence begins thus:
*The gray-eyed morn smiles at the frowning night,*
*Checkering the Eastern skies with streaks of light.*
Now, how would you say this?"

Kevin frowned. "Let's see. I'd probably say something like:
*The sun comes up in the East.*
Or something like that."

"I see. Why would I go to all that trouble to say 'the sun comes up in the East' with the words I used?"

"Well, your words sound better. They're more ... musical, I think. And my way doesn't tell the audience how Friar Laurence feels about the morning. So, I guess your way has more ... stuff ... you know, meaning in it."

"Exactly! So why do students find my words boring? Why would they rather that I had expressed my thoughts your way?"

"I guess because it's poetry. Students don't like poetry."

"But why?"

"Well, poetry sounds phony."

"Phony? Pray tell, what do you mean?"

"Artificial. Not natural. But when you say your words, they sound natural, like you're speaking regular speech."

William smiled. "I will torment you no longer. The words must be grand, not everyday words, because our story is grand. The words must carry the story above the common place. But — and this is important to the actor — the grand words must be spoken in such a way that he who hears them finds them perfectly natural. The hearer must also feel that there is no finer way to express such thoughts, such feelings. I will give you my entire philosophy of acting. I included it in our next play, *Hamlet*, precisely because I wearied of actors ruining my words. It is part of a speech by Hamlet to a band of players who are to perform at the castle:

*Speak the speech, I pray you, as I pronounced to you, trippingly on the tongue, for if you mouth it, as many of our players do, I would as lief the town crier spoke my lines. Nor do not saw the air thus, but suit the action to the word, the word to the action. For it is the goal of playing to hold, as it 'twere, the mirror up to Nature.*

Now, do you see?"

"Yes, I see. You make it sound so natural, but the words are so wonderful."

William sighed. "I suspect that your teachers do not have the gift of actorly expression, or that my plays are treated as dusty books that have no life. Well, no matter. You and a few others in each generation can correct that. That, I presume, is my purpose in teaching you. Now, let us return to our play. The story is gathering speed."

# CHAPTER ELEVEN

The coach motioned to Kevin to join him in the dugout. Kevin had just finished infield practice.

"Kevin," the coach said, "I think I'll just play you for a couple of innings today. We're not up against much of a team, and I don't want to take any chances. Let's not run the risk of getting your beak bashed again."

"Fine, Coach. I'm a bit rusty anyway."

"Okay, let's let you have two at-bats and sit you down. How's that sound?"

"Sure," Kevin said.

Kevin singled both times he was at bat. After he scored the second time, he returned to the dugout and asked the coach, "Coach, is it alright if I sit in the stands with my parents? Would you mind?"

"Naw," said the coach, "you go ahead. You had a good game, and I can't put you back in anyway. Just be sure to yell loud for us."

Kevin joined his parents in the bleachers, who were sitting with William. "Nice game," Mr. Ryan said. "Good hitting."

"Thanks, Dad. So, William, how do you like your first baseball game?"

"Very interesting. I was just saying to your mother that it resembles an old game — a very old game — that we play at home. Rounders, it is called. Very similar. Yet different enough to make the adventure rather stimulating."

"Mr. Kemp was particularly interested in you, Kevin. I believe he lost his dignity for a moment when you got that last hit." Kevin's mother was smiling, and obviously pleased that her son's tutor was proud of his pupil

"Yes, indeed," said William. "You are indeed graceful, and clearly gifted at the sport. But let me see if I have captured the essence of the game. The goal of the hurler, I believe, is to keep the man with the cudgel from striking the ball. The object of the — what is it you call him? The batter? — fellow with the cudgel is to defy the hurler and strike the ball into the nether regions of the playing area. Am I correct thus far?"

"Right on, Mr. Kemp," Mr. Ryan said.

"Now, striking the ball is in itself not sufficient. The ball must elude the other players who support the hurler. It must fall onto the playing field, and the batter must reach one of the white pillows strategically arranged on the playing field. When batters have advanced each of his successful fellows who went before him, so that he reaches the object that is pentagonal, the team has scored. It appears that three unsuccessful attempts by batters result in a change of sides, and the game continues thus. Do I grasp its essence?"

"That's marvelous, Mr. Kemp!" said Mrs. Ryan. "You should be a sports caster."

"I beg your pardon?" William said.

"My mother thinks that you are so good at explaining the game that you should report it on television," said Kevin.

"Indeed? Well, thank you very much, Mrs. Ryan. I shall be more attentive when I encounter this game on television. Imagine. A sports caster. How very interesting." William absent-mindedly reached into his bag of popcorn. "But there is one element of which I am not clear. When is the game over?"

"Oh," Mr. Ryan said, "When each side has been up nine times. Whoever has the most runs is the winner."

William frowned. "Why nine? How did they arrive at that rather odd number?"

The Ryans looked blankly at one another. Finally, Mr. Ryan said, "I don't know. I guess whoever invented the game liked the number nine."

"Ah, I see. One of the mysteries residing in the far-off history of the sport. Such oddities always puzzle me. I find myself wanting to know the reason for such things. Ah, well, there are some things we are not meant to know, aren't there?"

# CHAPTER TWELVE

Only eight days remained. On July 1$^{st}$ , William would disappear to wherever he had come from. Kevin was troubled because he didn't want William to leave. He looked forward eagerly to their daily sessions. When he wasn't at baseball practice — held in the early mornings to avoid the heat of the day — or playing in his twice-weekly baseball games, Kevin was in the public library, preparing for his class with William or reading everything he could find on Shakespeare.

They were now working on *Hamlet*. This was a more complicated play than *Romeo and Juliet*, and Kevin often struggled to understand what was going on. William was patient with him, and Kevin began to enjoy the difficulties of the play.

One day, when they had paused in their study of the play, Kevin suddenly asked William, "Tell me, William, if you don't mind, how often did you take a bath when ... you were alive?"

"Bath? Yes, that is an odd question. Well, I can tell you Kevin, that I was an exception. I bathed everyday. Very few people in my time did so. There was seldom water that was hot, and it took a great deal of determination to engage in the practice. I was considered quite strange by my associates, but I persevered. I truly believed that cleanliness was indeed next to godliness. Now that you mention it, I must tell you of my first appearance on a stage. I entered — I had a very small role — and I was struck by the stench, the fearful odor emanating from the audience. I had to speak my few lines directly to them, and all I could think of is how terrible they smelled. No, Kevin, my age was not a pleasant one when it came to the odors of life. Why do you ask?"

"Well, I've been reading about the 'Age of Shakespeare,' and ..."

William interrupted. "I am gratified that you call it thus, but it is more correctly the 'Age of Elizabeth'."

"Anyway," Kevin continued, "it seems a lot more unpleasant than I had thought. Nobody washed, there was garbage and sewage in the streets, and people lived all crowded together."

"In London, yes, but in the countryside it was not thus. My ties to Stratford were for the very reasons of which you speak. Fresh air, country life, comparative cleanliness. That is why I was always drawn to Stratford, and why I chose to return there again and again, and, I might add, to retire there."

"There's another thing," Kevin said. "What is all this stuff about your not writing the plays? That someone else was Shakespeare."

"Ah, we have come to that, have we? I am aware of such ideas. Allow me to explain. Most of the playwrights of my day were university trained. Some of the nobility dabbled in playwrighting. It seems that some folk find it difficult that a young man from the country could have the education and the experiences to have written my plays. They are wrong, of course. I had a quite competent education, and I have taught myself much, just as you are teaching yourself. There is, in brief, no substance to such claims, although they persist."

"Doesn't that make you angry?" Kevin asked.

"No, of course not. I know what I have done. I leave it to others to concern themselves on such matters. Now, enough of this. Let us return to our play. We are at an important point in the play. Now ..."

*To be ... or not to be. That is the question.*

*Whether 'tis nobler in the mind to suffer the slings and arrows of outrageous fortune,*

*Or to take arms against a sea of troubles,*

*And by opposing end them.*

"I understand it!" Kevin almost shouted. "It makes sense! The way you say the lines, it makes sense! Hamlet's trying to figure out if he wants to live, if he wants to put up with all the stuff he's had to put up with."

William smiled. "What did it mean to you before that?"

"They were just words — just a jumble of words."

"Ah, I see the problem. One must seek the meaning in the lines, not merely recite the words. You know, Kevin, this is my most famous soliloquy, and …"

"What's a soliloquy?" Kevin interrupted.

Well, you see, a soliloquy is a speech in which the character reveals his thoughts, his feelings, to the audience. Until my actors performed my plays, soliloquies were merely speeches declaimed to the audience. They are much more than that. In a sense, the actor must be unaware of the audience, if the soliloquy is to reveal the innermost nature of the character."

"I see," said Kevin. "They're not supposed to be something out of an opera or something."

"Exactly, my boy. Now, I must confess that this is not my favorite soliloquy in the play. We will come to that. As it is, I am rather proud of it, but it is not the best. And, I might add, this is my favorite play, but not my greatest. I reserve that honor for *King Lear*. It is — *Hamlet*, I mean — my most interesting play."

"Why is that?"

"It is because I created these characters in a certain way, but each time it is performed, they surprise me. Every character, even the most minor, changes with the nature of the actor. It is as if I have created characters who have lives of their own, independent of the author. It is quite wonderful. You see, one other adventure I am permitted is to be allowed to attend new performances of *Hamlet* as they are produced throughout time. I have seen, I would venture, several hundred productions of the play, and I continue to be amazed.

Kevin thought for a moment. "I can see how that could be. Sometimes, while I'm reading the play, Hamlet seems like a guy who can't make up his mind. Sometimes he seems as if he knows what he's doing, and he's following out some kind of plan. He's a hard guy to figure out."

"Aren't we all, Kevin? Aren't we all."

# CHAPTER THIRTEEN

Julia and Kevin had just come out of The Gap and were walking past the stores on the upper level of the mall. Kevin put his hand on Julia's arm and stopped. He pointed to the high glass ceiling of the mall, covering the large, planted center of the building. Shoppers thronged the corridors that radiated out from the center.

"Look. William says that our shopping malls are the modern versions of cathedrals. When you look at all of this from up here, it seems right. Shopping malls are our cathedrals."

Julia nodded. "Your Mr. Kemp is just about the smartest man I've ever met. I mean, who else who you've ever met would compare shopping malls and cathedrals?"

Kevin said, "You know, I think you'd enjoy *Hamlet*. Why don't you read it over the weekend and come to my tutoring session on Monday? Then you'll really see William in action."

"Do you think he'd mind?" Julia asked.

"Naw, he likes an audience. He's the best teacher I've ever had. He may be the best teacher who ever lived! Anyway, meet us at one of the umbrella tables outside the coffee shop. Two thirty."

"Okay. I'd like that."

Julia and Kevin were already sitting outside the coffee shop when William arrived. "Ah, the beauteous Julia! How delightful! Have you come to join us in our endeavors?" Without waiting for her to answer, he continued on. "A propitious moment to join our studies, fair Julia. We are at the very moment in the play when we are to examine the perplexing behavior of Ophelia. Are you familiar with the scene? The so-called 'mad scene,' wherein she loses her reason?"

"Yes. I read the play yesterday. I have to admit that I didn't understand a lot of it."

William waved his hand in a cheerful dismissal. "No matter. All shall be clear to you. At least, a bit clearer. I am not certain that this play ever becomes really clear. Now, Kevin, outline the situation for us. What has happened to deprive Ophelia of her sanity?"

"Well, her brother has gone to France. Hamlet — well, she thought that Hamlet loved her, but he rejects her. He's pretty mean with her. And then, to top things off, Hamlet kills her father, thinking that the old man is his uncle, King Claudius. So, she goes crazy."

"Good, very good. A very nice summary. Now, do you think she killed herself, or was it an accident?"

Kevin was silent for a moment. "I don't know. Maybe she killed herself. But then maybe she just fell into the river. I guess I think that she didn't know what she was doing or where she was, and she just kind of slipped in, floated for awhile, and sank."

"That is my problem, and I wrote the play! I do not really know myself. That is the fascination I have with my own characters. But, you see, it is very like life itself. One never knows for certain what inspires people to do what they do. One can only communicate the strangeness of action, and never really grasp the motive. Do you see what I mean?"

Kevin looked surprised. "Don't you plot out what happens? I mean, don't you try to figure out in advance why something happens?"

"Ah, yes, to a degree. But I prefer to allow my characters to lead me down the path of my plot. I will create a sequence in the broadest of terms, and then I allow the character to tell me what he or she would like to do. Or, in the case of Hamlet himself, what he would not like to do. Think about it. It would be a poor play indeed if the audience can easily predict what will unfold. On the other hand, the actions must not be so improbable that the audience feels deceived. It is a fine line. My approach is to allow the logic of the plot to follow the nature of the characters involved in it. I trust that you find that this method is satisfactory?"

"I see what you mean. Hamlet and Ophelia and all the rest are kind of caught up in things that are beyond their control, so what they do seems logical, even when it surprises us."

"Excellent! And the tragedy is all the greater when both events and flaws in their own natures come together. Now, fair Julia. I am curious to learn what you think of Gertrude, wife of the murdered king, wife of his brother and slayer of her first husband, and mother of the troubled Hamlet. What say you of her?"

Julia had been wide-eyed during the entire session and had said little. This was the first time that William had asked her a question directly. She was also confused.

"I'm not sure I've been getting this. Kevin, you talk as if Mr. Kemp wrote these plays. I mean, you're talking about him as if he actually was William Shakespeare!"

Kevin blushed. He was about to respond to Julia when William said, "This must come as something of a surprise to you, dear Julia, but I am indeed he. I am William Shakespeare. Kevin and I quite forgot ourselves. You see, Kevin knows of my true self, and we have been studying my plays in the full light of that knowledge. You, of course, must perceive such a revelation as sheer madness. I must ask you to suspend your alarm for the while. Even if I am a middle-aged madman, does it not strike you that I have special knowledge of the subject? That we can, for the moment, accept the special knowledge as an indication of a particularly effective and, as it were, gentle madness? As your physicians would say, I am quite harmless. Now, for the purposes of our study of the play, I again ask you: What of Gertrude?"

Julia looked at Kevin, who smiled back at her and nodded. She wasn't sure what to think. Whatever Mr. Kemp was, he certainly was a great teacher. She swallowed, and said, "I feel sorry for her."

"Sorry?" William exclaimed. "She wasn't very loyal to Hamlet's father."

"Oh, I know," Julia said. "But think of it. She's probably still pretty young. I mean, women had children when they were very young in those days, didn't they, Mr. Kemp?"

"Please. You may call me William. We are, after all, friends. Now, as to Gertrude, yes, very young. Often as young as yourself. Often before they had attained an age of fifteen."

"So, here we have a woman who is not much over forty, if that, who is suddenly a widow, and we have the smooth Claudius move in on her, and ..."

"I beg your pardon? 'Move in on her.' Could you explain that?"

"Sweet talk her," Julia said. "Sweep her off her feet. You know."

"I believe I do. Go on," William said.

Julia frowned. "She certainly cares for Hamlet, but she doesn't have the faintest idea of how to help him out of his sadness. She likes the idea of Hamlet and Ophelia getting together, even if Ophelia's father, Polonius, doesn't like the idea. And she's completely blown away when Hamlet yells at her so ferociously in her bed chamber, particularly when he sees a ghost that she can't see. Finally, she has to put up with Hamlet being sent away to England and her hopes for Hamlet and Ophelia gone when Ophelia dies. So, all in all, I kind of feel sorry for her. I think she meant well, but she made a mistake in marrying Claudius."

"Ah very good. Very perceptive. I tend to agree with your assessment. Do you think that Gertrude knew that she had made a mistake?"

"Pretty sure. I think that she knows that there's poison in the cup intended for Hamlet, and that she drinks it anyway. That's what makes her tragic. She pays for her mistake by doing a brave thing."

"William smiled. "The both of you are very satisfactory pupils. We shall stop there. A most productive session, my dears. I look forward to tomorrow with eagerness. But, I must be off. I need to rest before your baseball contest this evening, Kevin. Such displays of athletic combat quite exhaust me, and I must be ready to cheer you on. Until this evening, then, my children. Adieu."

# CHAPTER FOURTEEN

The pitch was six inches outside. Kevin threw his bat toward the dugout and started for first base.

"Strike three!" the umpire shouted, snapping his right arm in the air.

Kevin looked back at the umpire, Mr. Berger, a big teddy-bear of a man. He smiled, and headed for the dugout. The crowd booed its disapproval.

Suddenly, above the noise of the crowd, a voice rang out, clear and theatrical.

"Oh, a most grievous error, Master Umpire!"

Coach Minetti, hurrying from the dugout for a confrontation with Mr. Berger, stopped in his tracks. Kevin, fearful that his coach and the umpire were about to get into an argument, was right behind Mr. Minetti, ready to restrain him.

Coach turned to Kevin. "What the heck was that? Kurt," he said to Mr. Berger, "did you hear that?"

Holding his mask in his hand, Mr. Berger walked up to the coach and Kevin. "I think I just got told off. If I did, it was the grandest razzberry I ever got."

"That's my tutor, Mr. Berger. He's English. He's kinda new to the game, and he must have gotten carried away."

Coach Minetti scowled. "Geez, Kurt, that pitch was half a foot outside."

"Yeah, I know, Sal. I missed it. It happens, y'know."

By this time, the crowd, expecting a spectacular argument between the coach and the umpire, was again booing and clapping. "Look, Kurt, I gotta do something. We just can't stand here. It'll make me look bad."

"You could kick some dirt, Coach. Maybe throw your hat down. Then I could drag you away," Kevin said.

Coach looked at Mr. Berger. "That okay with you, Kurt?"

"Sure, only don't drag it out. I want to finish this game before eight, if we can. Oh, Kevin, what did he say again? I gotta tell my wife. What'd he say?"

"I think it was, 'Oh, what a grievous error, Master Umpire,' or something like that."

"That's beautiful," Mr. Berger said. "Really beautiful. Okay Sal. Kick your dirt and let's get back to the game."

Coach dramatically kicked the dirt around home plate, threw his hat down and stomped on it, all while Mr. Berger, his back turned away from Coach and Kevin, looked up at the stands, his arms folded. The crowd loved it. Finally, Kevin took Coach by the arm and forced him back to the dugout.

"Play ball!" Mr. Berger shouted, and the game resumed.

Kevin doubled his next time up, walked the following time on the same pitch that Mr. Berger had called him out on in the first inning, and then singled his last time up.

"Nice game, Mr. Berger," Kevin said as the teams were leaving the field.

"Thanks, Kevin. That's nice of you, considering. Still — I hope you don't mind — it was worth it. I never been so proud of goofing up in all my years of umpiring."

After Kevin had showered and changed, he was met at the clubhouse door by his parents, Mr. and Mrs. Black, Julia, and William. "Good game, son," Mr. Ryan said.

"Quite splendid, Kevin. I hope that my exclamation caused you no embarrassment. I was overcome with the excitement of the contest."

"No problem, William. I think you made Mr. Berger and Coach's day. They were impressed. They'd never heard a more literate heckle."

Mr. Black laughed. "That's for sure," he said. "Okay, now where are we off to for this birthday dinner? Where'd you pick for us, Jim?"

"I thought we'd try the Sir Walter Raleigh Steak House. Sound okay to you, Kevin?"

"Great," he said.

"An odd name for an eating place," William said.

Julia and Kevin both began to laugh. "What's so funny, you two?" asked Mrs. Ryan.

William replied. "I believe, Mrs. Ryan, that the young people are amused that we would be celebrating Kevin's birthday named after an old friend of mine. Yes, it is curious. Is this what one would call a coincidence, Kevin? Well, no matter. I look forward to the celebration. A place so named must have excellent beef."

# CHAPTER FIFTEEN

"And that, Kevin, is that. In the brief time we have had, I can do no more. Tomorrow I must leave you."

William reached down into his briefcase, a worn tan leather bag that was sealed with a clasp. He reached in and removed a small, velvet-covered box about the size of a deck of cards. He laid it on the table before Kevin.

"I had no opportunity to give you this last night at your very festive birthday dinner, Kevin. I would like you to have this."

"What is it?"

"Ah, that you will only discover when you open it, won't you? Go ahead."

Kevin opened the box. Inside was a small portrait within a delicate gold frame. It was of a young man, dressed in Elizabethan clothes, a stiff lace collar lying on his shoulders. He had reddish-brown hair, a small, wispy beard, and a slight smile. Kevin looked at the portrait, then at William.

"I fear it is not a very exciting gift for a young man of fifteen years. Perhaps you are disappointed."

Kevin shook his head. "No, it's just that … it's just that I've never had a present like this." Kevin continued to look at the miniature portrait. He looked up at William again. "It's you, isn't it?"

"You caught the resemblance? Yes, when I was young. I believe I was about twenty-six or so. It is by Nicholas Hilliard. Quite a good likeness, don't you think?"

"You mean I have a portrait of William Shakespeare when he was young?"

"Indeed you do. Although over the years you will remember it only as an interesting gift of an antique work of art. I want you to have it. There were only four copies of it made. One is in the National Portrait Gallery in London, one in the Folger Shakespeare Library in Washington, and two whose whereabouts are unknown. Actually, I know where they are.

You have one, and I, the other. I do not wish to appear immodest, but I believe what I have given you is quite valuable."

"It's great, William. Really great."

"Let us not be unduly sentimental. My thought is that it could provide, one day, the means by which you will be able to pay for your university education, and perhaps give you a start in life. It is, in effect, an endowment. More than that, it is my expression of my confidence in your eventual success."

"Hey, I'd never sell it!"

"You may have to. Do not think that you must keep it for my sake. It should be used to further your future. It is, after all, merely an object."

"It's more than that, William. It's the most important thing I own."

"Let me tell you what will happen with it. I can tell you that much. You will show it to your parents and Julia, and they will remark on it as being unique and — as they will put it — interesting. You will place it carefully in a drawer, and a few years from now, you will discover that you have it. At that time, circumstances will dictate what you do with it. If it can help you, all the better. If you do not need to capitalize on its value, that is fine. The important thing is that I want you to have it, so that in your necessary forgetting of me, a small gleam of vague remembrance will persist."

"I won't forget you, William. I don't see how that's possible," Kevin said.

"Oh, you will forget me, Kevin, it must be. However, deep in your memory, you will not. For that, I thank the powers that propel me. Well, enough of this."

Kevin stirred the ice in the bottom of his plastic cup with his straw. "What's to become of me, William?"

"How do you mean? You shall continue with your very interesting life. But now, you shall have some understanding of matters that you did not heretofore have."

"Yes, but what will I be?"

"Be? You shall be yourself."

"You know what I mean. You know what my future is, don't you?"

"Ah, I do indeed. It is not something I can tell you, however. One must not live one's life with foreknowledge. It is not the natural state of things. As I told you, you will remember that one summer you were instructed by an odd tutor, but you will not remember who I am. Then you will proceed with your destiny, as you make it."

"What about Julia? I haven't told her who you are, but I think she knows."

William smiled. "Yes, I am not surprised. A very intelligent and perceptive young woman. And delightfully curious. But, no, she will not remember her suspicions. I can tell you that the two of you will remain ... connected. But I can say no more."

Kevin sighed. "It doesn't seem fair. I've been taught by Shakespeare, and I won't even remember it."

This time William laughed. "There are more things in heaven and earth, Horatio, then are dreamt of in your philosophy."

Then Kevin laughed as well. "Yeah, I guess so."

"But Kevin, my boy, what do *you* see for your future? That is the question. Surely you will go to university, a young man of your abilities."

"Oh, sure. I take the SATs this fall, and then the year after that, I'll apply to some colleges." Kevin paused. "You know, William, I think I'd like to be an actor. I mean, being a Shakespeare scholar and all that stuff is interesting, but I think I'd like to help — I dunno — make the plays come alive, if you know what I mean."

"I do, indeed. It has always disturbed me that I have had my plays turned into literature, rather than for what they were intended. Yes, you shall be an actor. And a very fine one, I'll warrant."

"What do I have to do?"

"A good question. You must continue to examine the plays — not only mine, but those of every considerable writer of plays — and be taught by acting masters. You must learn to fence, to dance, to train your voice. Most important, you must always remember my advice to the actors. Do you remember? 'Speak the speech, I pray you...' All of that will serve you well."

"I suppose you have to go."

"Yes, I must. But, take heart. We shall see each other at least one more time. You won't remember who I am, but I venture that there will be an occasion when we will meet again."

"When I play Hamlet?" Kevin asked.

William raised his eyebrows. "You *are* a clever boy. I cannot tell you. But I will see you again. Please give my fondest best wishes to the charming Julia, and your very fine parents. I will not shake your hand. It is too final. Let us say that I must be on my way to my next assignment, wherever and whenever that may be. We will keep in touch. You see, whenever you read one of my plays, or see one performed, we will be in communication. Now, enough of this. I must be off. Farewell for now, Kevin."

They both stood, and for a moment looked at one another, as if they were trying to memorize each other's face. Then, impulsively, Kevin came forward and hugged William.

"See ya around, William," Kevin said.

William smiled, gave a gentle wave of his hand, and walked jauntily away.

# CHAPTER SIXTEEN

There was still an evening remaining, before William had to leave. As he walked into Black's Hardware Store, he waved to Mr. Black. "I say, good landlord, I wonder if you would like to accompany me this evening. It is, after all, my last night in your fair town, and I would like to spend it with good friends."

Mr. Black smiled. He had never gotten used to Mr. Kemp's strange way of talking. "Sure, I suppose so. A little pub-crawling? Is that what you have in mind?"

"Indeed, but one pub shall be sufficient. And I fear that 'crawling,' as you phrase it, is not a very good idea. No, a few libations and some good conversation is what I seek."

"Would you like me to see if Jim Ryan is free?" asked Mr. Black.

"Splendid idea! By all means! The three of us shall contemplate the mysteries of life in a convivial setting. Say, eight o'clock?"

"That's fine. I'll call Jim. Shall we meet at O'Grady's?"

"Wonderful! Well, till then. I shall retire, and be fresh for our adventure." With a wave, William turned and left.

As John Black and Jim Ryan walked into O'Grady's, they were hailed from a corner booth by William. "Over here, Gentlemen. I have secured a quiet spot for our modest revelries." He stood and motioned them to their chairs. "What shall we have? Some of your fine American ale? My good young lady, please fetch us a pitcher of your best ale, and three tankards. Thank you very much, dear lady."

"So," Mr. Ryan said, "John tells me we are to contemplate the mysteries of life. I didn't know there were that many mysteries to contemplate. I mean, besides birth and death, what else is there?"

"Everything in between," Mr. Black said. "Everything in between is a mystery to you, isn't it, Mr. Kemp?"

"Ah, call me William, please. Indeed everything in between is a mystery. Or should I say 'mysteries?' One following another."

"Tell me, William, what do you think of my boy, my Kevin? Do you think that he has what it takes?"

"Has what it takes? Oh, I see. Does he have the potential to succeed in this dreary thing we call Life? Indeed he does. He is not only uncommonly intelligent, but he is sensitive without being vulnerable, quick without being irresponsible. He is a most unusual young man."

"We've always thought so. Sometimes I've worried that he's too good."

"That surprises me, Jim," Mr. Black said. "One of the things I thank the Lord for every day is that Julia doesn't give me a minute's worry. You should be grateful."

"I know, I know," Mr. Ryan said. "But I'm not sure people — you know the kind I mean — like boys like Kevin much. You know, they're jealous of him."

William said, "I understand your fears, Jim, but, you see, it doesn't matter to Kevin. Oh, I do not mean that he is indifferent to how others see him. Indeed, he cares very much for their approval. But he has confidence in who he is, so that any doubts expressed by others can be examined objectively by him. I predict wonderful accomplishments for him, and I believe that he will be highly esteemed."

"Let's get back to the mysteries of Life, William. Here's what's been bothering me. How can humans — you and me and Jim here — pretend to be civilized, and yet you can see so much cruelty every day? Is it just human nature or something?"

William smiled sadly. "It is human nature, my friend. Men are cruel, jealous, resentful, and, I am sad to say, in some cases simply evil. One could wish that all men — and women — were kind and civil, but then we would have no art, no literature, no drama. I have my theory. You see, in order to grow as humans, we must face our inner demons and those of others. As you say, they are part of our nature. Our nature required us to be cruel in order to survive. Our task in Life is to nurture our better natures over that which rendered us no greater than the lowly beast. I have seen ..." William stopped suddenly.

"What? What have you seen?" asked Mr. Ryan.

William looked down. "I have seen," he said quietly, "men hanged, their bodies desecrated. I have seen the fear in their eyes, their silent pleas for help — help which I could not render. I have seen disease so terrible that bodies were piled higher than a dwelling, creating beasts of those unaffected and still living. I have seen..." He paused again. All three men were silent.

Then, Mr. Black spoke up. "Where did you see all this, William? In your travels through time?" He said this seriously, not mockingly.

"What are you talking about? What travels through time?" Mr. Ryan was confused.

William sighed. "Yes, but more in my own time." He paused, and said, "Gentlemen, I am going to tell you who I am. Tomorrow, when I have gone, you will not remember what I have told you. You will remember only that you enjoyed a glass or two with Kevin's odd tutor. You see, the time of which I speak is the Age of Elizabeth — not the current queen, but the Great Queen. It is also the time of James the First, her successor. It is an age of glory, filth, cruelty, great minds, and much sadness. I can speak of these things, for I have lived through them. My name is not Kemp. Kevin knows this and Julia suspects it. It is William Shakespeare."

The two men looked at one another. Then, Mr. Ryan said, "That's interesting, William. That's ... nice."

Mr. Black said, "Yes, really nice."

William smiled at them. "I shall allow the two of you to contemplate this revelation whilst I avail myself of the facilities." He rose from his chair and headed for the Men's Room.

"That is one wacko man," Mr. Ryan said.

"Yeah, but he's harmless. Look, Jim, my advice is that we keep this to ourselves. From what Julia tells me, Kevin thinks the world of him, and he has been a good tutor to the boy. No sense ruining his admiration of the man."

Mr. Ryan took a sip of his beer. "If Kevin already knows that he's ... that he says he's Shakespeare, what difference would it make?"

"Oh, yeah, I see what you mean. Well, I guess if we don't tell the kids that we know what they know, then they won't think that we think that he's crazy. Do you follow me?"

"I think so. I guess you're right. No harm done, anyway. Okay, mum's the word."

After fifteen minutes, Mr. Black said, "Where is he? He's been gone an awfully long time."

"I'll go check," Mr. Ryan said.

He returned a minute or later. "He' not in the Men's Room. He's gone."

"Oh, Lord," Mr. Black said. "I hope he's not having one of his fits again. A few weeks ago, he kinda wandered off."

"Shall we go look for him?"

"No, he'll probably be all right. He gets confused, I think, and then seems to snap out of it. We'll wait awhile, and then I'll check to see if he's come home. Well, let's have another pitcher. My turn."

William did not return. When Mr. Black knocked gently at the door to William's apartment when he had arrived home, there was no answer. Quietly, he opened the door and softly whispered, "William?"

There was no answer. William Kemp — or Shakespeare — had gone.

# CHAPTER SEVENTEEN

It was a hectic time for Kevin. Tomorrow night he would perform in the University of Connecticut's production of *Hamlet*. Next week he had to submit his thesis for his Master's Degree. The following week, after the performances of *Hamlet* were finished, he and Julia were to be married. In a little less than three weeks, Kevin would have gone from student to graduate to husband.

Julia noticed that Kevin seemed very calm about all of this. He rose early, went to his fencing lessons, worked on his thesis, went to rehearsals, and the two of them would go to a movie. By the time the day was over, it was often after midnight, but Kevin would be up by six a.m., ready to begin his day.

On Saturday afternoons, Kevin would play baseball for a team in Manchester, Connecticut, and on Sundays he and Julia would travel around the countryside, exploring small and historic towns.

When Kevin and Julia had entered the University of Connecticut in the fall of 1998, only Kevin knew what he wanted to do. He would major in Drama and English Literature. Julia was undecided, but she felt that she should major in something that would support the both of them, since there was no question that Kevin intended to be an actor, and the income of actors was always uncertain. She decided on a pre-law program, and found that she enjoyed it. As Kevin was finishing his Master's Degree, Julia was in her next to last year in law school. Rather than waiting until she graduated, they had decided to get married in November. While she finished her work over the next year or so, Kevin could commute to New York City and try for acting jobs. If he had to, he could get a teaching position while Julia finished her legal studies. Julia's parents would support them until Julia could find a job with a law firm after graduation, so Kevin's teaching might not have to occur.

Julia watched the final dress rehearsal of *Hamlet*. Other than the actor playing Polonius forgetting his lines at one point in the play, it went well. It was clear to Julia that Kevin was going to be a very successful professional actor.

"Aren't you exhausted?" Julia asked Kevin after the rehearsal.

"No, not a bit tired. I'm too excited to be tired. I can't tell you what it feels like to play Hamlet — to *be* Hamlet. It's like I'm inside someone else, and when the play's over, as if I've been born again, this time as Kevin. Weird, huh?"

"No. It does make sense. It sounds a lot like Mr. Kemp."

# CHAPTER EIGHTEEN

Kevin thought that he should be nervous. He wasn't, not in the least. He was excited, that was for sure, but he wasn't nervous. He had lived with this play, with the part of Hamlet, for over eight years, since that summer when he was first introduced to it by his tutor. Kevin knew every word, every gesture, every detail of his part, including how he would feel when he spoke his lines.

He was a funny little man, William Kemp, but the greatest teacher Kevin had ever had. Somehow, tonight would be the proof that he had been taught well, that summer of his fifteenth birthday.

The theatre was the largest that Kevin had ever performed in. The audience, the stage manager told him, was a full house, some six hundred. It wasn't that common to have a full house for a play at the University of Connecticut's Katter Theatre, but word had spread that there was a young man playing the role of Hamlet who was sensational. How this word had spread was a mystery to Kevin, since very few people who were not connected with the production had seen rehearsals of the play.

"Places," the stage manager called. "Curtain in five minutes."

Kevin could hear the murmur of the audience. He found his place stage right, where he would sneak on in the dark in Scene Two, to take his place in the first court scene. He breathed deeply and closed his eyes.

The lights went down slowly, than completely out. The actors for Scene One took their places. It wasn't a theatre with a curtain, but a thrust stage, a large platform that jutted out into the audience, so that the audience was on three sides of the action. Softly the music began, than faded, the lights came up. The play began.

"Who's there? Stand and reveal yourself."

The first scene on the battlements of Elsinore proceeded. Marcellus and Bernardo talked, and then they were joined by Horatio. The Ghost of Hamlet's father appeared, and then disappeared. The scene ended.

In the dark stage hands dressed all in black placed two thrones at the back of the stage, and rolled a long red carpet from the thrones to just short of the front of the platform. The lights faded up, and Scene Two began.

Shortly into Scene Two, after the King, Claudius, had spoken to the assembled courtiers about the death of his brother, his marriage to his brother's wife, the Queen, Gertrude, he spoke to Hamlet.

"How goes it with our cousin, Hamlet?"

Kevin spoke his first lines, softly but clearly, away from the King and Queen and towards the audience.

"A little more than kin and less than kind."

Three hours later, when the lights had gone out at the end of the play, there was a hush in the audience. The applause began slowly, as if the audience was reluctant to break the spell, and then rose to a mighty sound. The lights slowly came back on, and in groups the actors appeared for their bows, until only one actor had not appeared.

From the very back of the stage Kevin walked briskly to the very front, bowed, and stepped back to hold hands with the actors who had played Claudius and Gertrude. The applause was deafening. The three actors bowed again, and then joined hands with the actors who had played Polonius, Laertes, and Ophelia. The line of six actors bowed once more, and the applause continued. Then the actors, in groups, left the stage, leaving the six principals, and then all but Kevin left. He stepped forward, bowed, and looked up.

In the front row of the narrow balcony that formed a horseshoe around the audience area stood a slight man with a reddish, pointed beard. He was smiling broadly, applauding lustily. Kevin saw him and was frozen for a moment. Then, smiling back, he turned slightly in the direction of the man in the balcony, and bowed again.